ERIKA – SAN

Allen Say

Houghton Mifflin Books for Children
Houghton Mifflin Harcourt
Boston 2009

www.hmhbooks.com

Houghton Mifflin Books for Children is an imprint
of Houghton Miffflin Harcourt Publishing Company.

The text of this book is set in Centaur.
The illustrations are done in watercolor.

Library of Congress Cataloging-in-Publication Data

Say, Allen.
Erika-san / written and illustrated by Allen Say.
p. cm.
Summary: After falling in love with Japan as a little girl, Erika becomes a teacher and fulfills her
childhood dream by moving to a remote Japanese island.
ISBN 978-0-618-88933-4
[I. Japan—Fiction.] I. Title.
PZ7.S2744Er 2008
[E]—dc22
2008000601

Printed in Singapore
TWP 10 9 8 7 6 5 4 3 2 1

For

URSALA-SAN

In her grandmother's house, framed pictures hung in the hallway. One of them showed a cottage with lighted windows. Erika would remember the picture all her life.

"I want to live there," she said the first time she saw it.

"It's an old print, darling," Grandmother said. "Grandpa bought it in Japan when he was a young man."

"I want to go there when I grow up," Erika said.

And since that day, Erika wanted to know more about Japan, so Grandmother checked out Japanese picture books and folktales from the library and read them to her at bedtime.

Erika made many friends—some of them Japanese—and learned to say "konnichiwa" for "hello" and "sayonara" for "goodbye" and many other words besides. She studied Japanese in middle school and in high school and all the way through college.

The day Erika graduated, she was the first to say goodbye to all her friends.

"What's the hurry? Aren't you coming to the party?" they asked.

"Sayonara, everybody—I've got a teaching job in Tokyo!"

But when Erika arrived in Tokyo, she could not remember a single word of Japanese.

"Oh, dear," she sighed. "This isn't a city . . . it's a hundred cities all crammed together! And everything looks so new. Am I going to find my house here?"

She telephoned the agency that had found the job for her.

"Where is old Japan?" she asked. "I want to work in a smaller city."

"There is another job about three hours by the bullet train," the agent told her.

"I'll take it!" Erika said.

Erika struggled to the bullet train platform.

Now I'm in a space station, she thought. And here comes the rocket. This is going to take me to old Japan? Really, it feels more like I'm on my way to Mars!

Three hours later she came to a small city with low buildings and temples and no skyscrapers.

"Well, this is more like what I expected," she said, smiling. "A kind of place for cottages with thatched roofs . . . so lovely and quiet . . . But it's *too* quiet. Where are the people?"

She wandered through the empty streets until she heard roars of voices like the crashing of waves.

"A football stadium? In Japan?"

Erika walked to the large town square, and there she was swallowed up in a huge crowd. People bumped and jostled her from all sides, shouting and clapping their hands.

They must have followed me from Tokyo, she thought.

She called the agency once again.

"Please send me to a quieter place," she pleaded with the agent.

"The only other opening we have is on a remote island. It's so out of the way that no one wants to go there."

"I will!" Erika said.

Erika arrived on the island the next morning.

"This looks promising," she told herself. "Forests and hills and green mountains . . . just the right background for a little house . . ."

She came to a restaurant named Kamome. "That's 'seagull,'" she said, and walked in. It was empty except for a man and woman working behind the counter.

"Are you open for business?" she asked.

"Oh, yes, of course. Please sit anywhere," they said, and bowed.

Erika sat at the counter and ate her lunch.

"This is the best miso soup I've ever had," she told them.

The woman served her another bowl. And the couple told her of the apartments in the neighborhood and how to get to the school where Erika was to teach. By the time she left, she was calling them Mama-san and Papa-san.

The next morning, from the moment Erika entered the schoolyard, a crowd of children surrounded her.

"Foreigner! Foreigner!" they chanted in singsong voices.

"Oh, dear," she sighed. Once again, Erika could not think of a single Japanese word. Then she heard the sound of a whistle.

"Stand back, children, stand back!" A man came running. "Please forgive us," he said, and bowed. "We get so few foreign visitors here that the children are most curious. We heard that you were coming and they've been very excited."

"I'm so glad to meet you. My name is Erika," she said.

"Oh, wonderful, you speak Japanese! I'm Akira Imai. Let me show you to the principal's office."

By lunchtime, all the students called her Erika Sensei. *Sensei* means "teacher." Mr. Imai called her Erika-san, and she called him Aki-san.

"I'd be very happy to give you a tour of the island over the weekend," Aki offered.

"I would love that." Erika bowed.

Early Saturday morning, Aki came with two bicycles. They rode through rice paddies with hills and mountains all around. They bicycled along the rocky seacoast with many coves and empty beaches.

"Everything is so green and lovely!" Erika exclaimed. "I think my grandfather must have visited a place like this."

"He was a soldier, then?" Aki asked.

"I'm not sure. I don't remember him," she answered.

On their way home one weekend, Erika stopped suddenly.

"Wait, Aki-san, what is that? Can we have a look?" she asked, pointing at a thatched roof in a clump of trees.

As they walked toward it, a cottage appeared. Erika covered her mouth with a hand.

"I can't believe it!" she said. "That is exactly like the house I've always wanted to live in!"

Aki gave her a puzzled look. "But that's not a house," he said. "It's a *tea-house.* See the sign under the roof? It's called the Evening Moon."

"A teahouse?" she whispered.

"Yes—people rent the place for tea ceremonies."

"Do you know how to do that? Do you attend tea ceremonies?"

"I went with my grandfather once. He liked tea; I like coffee."

Erika was silent on the way home.

On Monday, Erika came to work as usual and taught her classes as usual, but she didn't say much to Aki. She smiled and said good morning to him, nodded to him in the hallway, and said goodbye in the afternoon.

She acted the same way the next day, and the next. They didn't go bicycling that weekend.

Every day after school, Aki sat in his favorite coffee shop and wondered.

"Is Erika-san upset with me because I like coffee and don't know anything about tea ceremony?"

Two months went by without one bicycle trip.

"I don't think Erika-san is ever going to have coffee with me again . . ."

Then the very next afternoon a familiar voice called from the doorway.

"So this is where you've been hiding," Erika said. "How have you been, Aki-san?"

Aki stared.

"Remember that teahouse we saw together, the Evening Moon?" she asked.

Aki nodded.

"I'd love to see it again. Won't you meet me there this Saturday? Say, three o'clock?"

"Yes!" he said loudly. "Would you have a cup of coffee with me now?"

"I'd love to," she said, and sat down.

Aki arrived at the teahouse early, but Erika was already waiting for him. He swallowed a breath.

"Mama-san at Kamome helped me put it on," she said, and turned in a circle to show off her kimono. "Won't you come into my teahouse? It's ours for the afternoon."

Silently, Aki followed her.

"I've been taking lessons," she explained as she prepared the tea things. "I didn't tell you because I wanted to surprise you. And this is just a practice. I'm only a beginner."

"You look like an expert to me!" Aki finally spoke.

"My sensei tells me it will take years before I can be good at tea ceremony," Erika said.

"Does that mean you are going to stay here . . . for years?" he asked.

"Well, I've always wanted to live in a teahouse, haven't I? So, don't you think I should be very good at making tea?"

"Yes!" he shouted. Then in a quiet tone he asked, "Would you mind very much if I came to your class? I have an old kimono that belonged to my grandfather."

"How wonderful. I'd love that!" she said.

They were married a year later. They found a small farmhouse on the
outskirts of town, nested in the green hillsides of old Japan.
And there Erika-san stayed, home at last.